FORTUNATELY

Written and illustrated by
REMY CHARLIP

Simon & Schuster   New York

Simon & Schuster Books for Young Readers
An imprint of Simon & Schuster Children's Publishing Division
1230 Avenue of the Americas, New York, New York 10020

Library of Congress Cataloging in Publication Data

Charlip, Remy.
  Fortunately.

  Summary: Good and bad luck accompany Ned from New York to Florida on his way to a surprise party.
  1. Children's stories, American. [1. Luck—Fiction]
I. Title.
PZ7.C3812Fo   1985   [E]   85-4493
ISBN 978-0-02-718100-5 (hc)
ISBN 978-0-689-71660-7 (pbk)
1111 SCP
Manufactured in China
10 9 8

**Fortunately
a friend loaned him an airplane.**

THIS BOOK IS DEDICATED TO NED AND CLAUDE AND THE PAPER BAG PLAYERS

Fortunately
one day, Ned got a letter that said,
"Please Come to a Surprise Party."

*But unfortunately
the party was in Florida
and he was in New York.*

Unfortunately
the motor exploded.

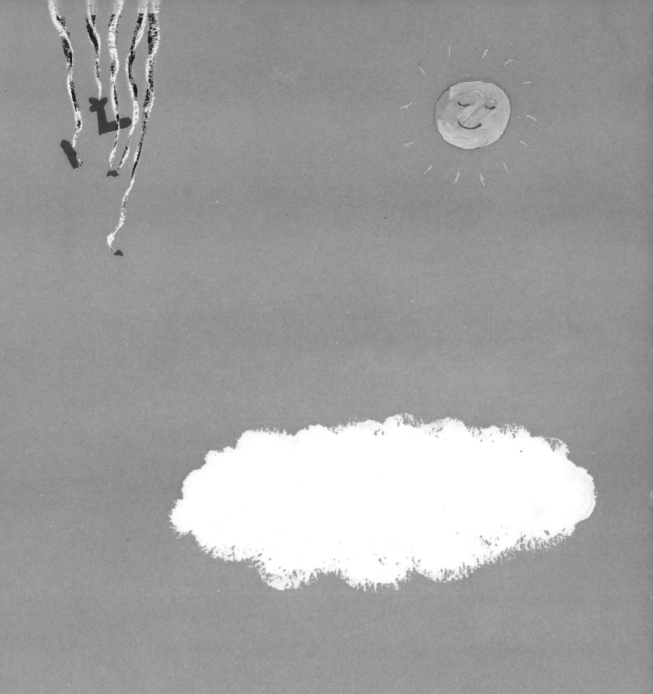

Fortunately
there was a parachute in the airplane.

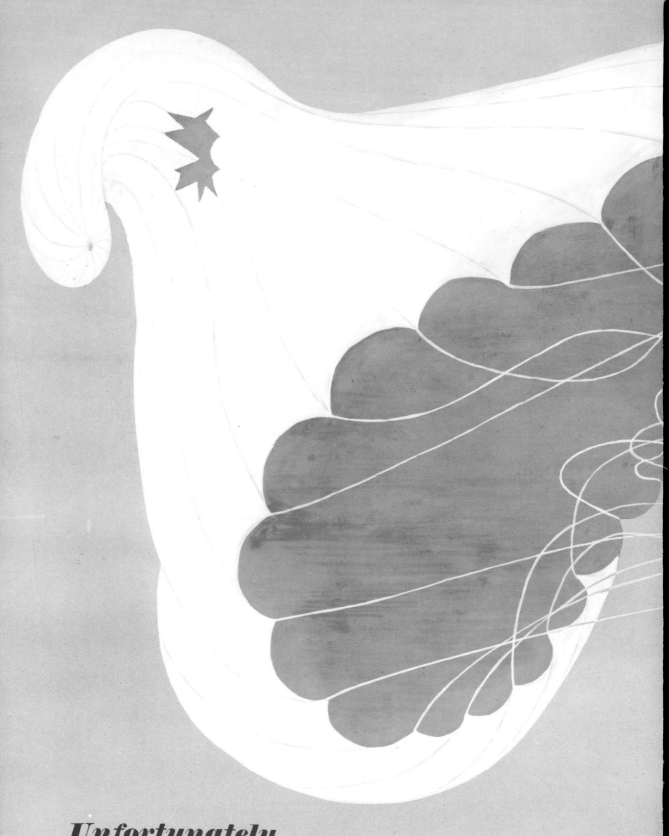

**Unfortunately
there was a hole in the parachute.**

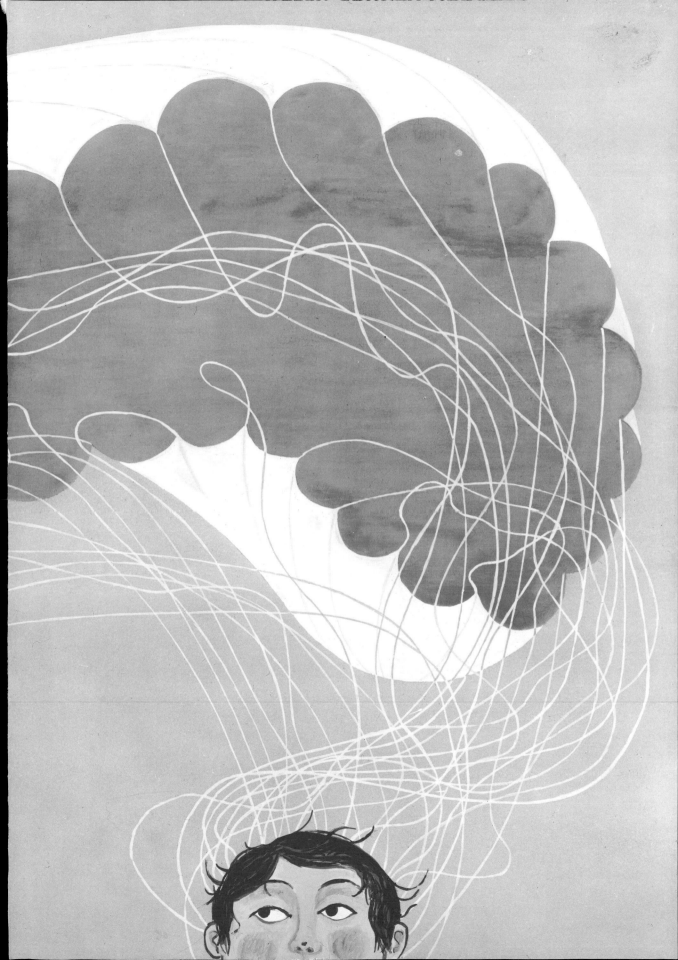

Fortunately
there was a haystack on the ground.

Unfortunately
there was a pitchfork in the haystack.

Fortunately
he missed the pitchfork.

**Unfortunately
he missed the haystack.**

Fortunately
he landed in water.

Unfortunately
there were sharks in the water.

*Fortunately
he could swim.*

Unfortunately
there were tigers on the land.

Fortunately
he could run.

Unfortunately
he ran into a deep dark cave.

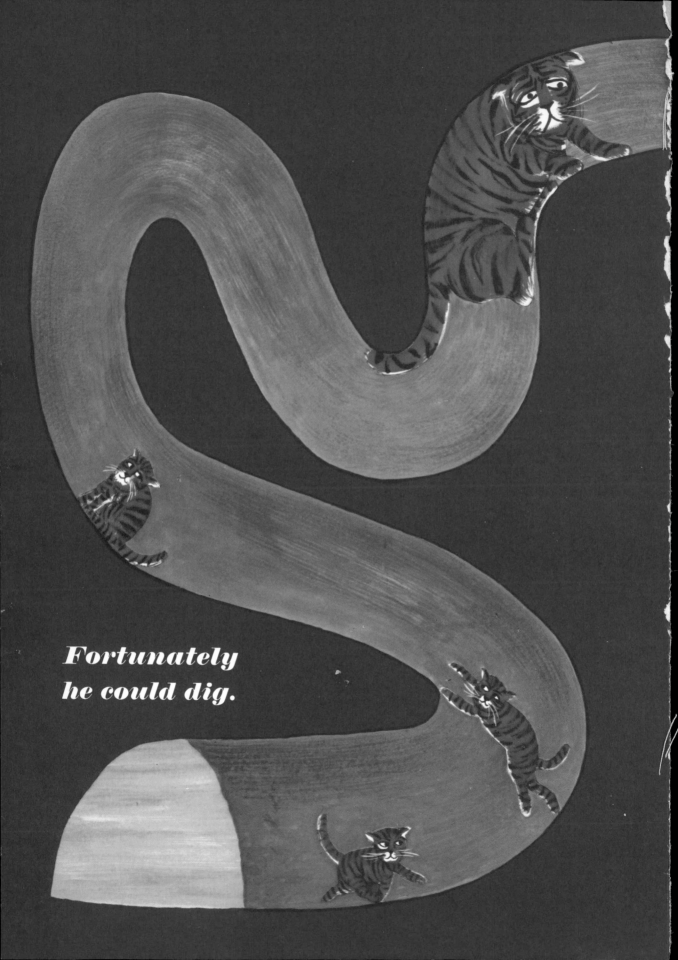

Fortunately he could dig.

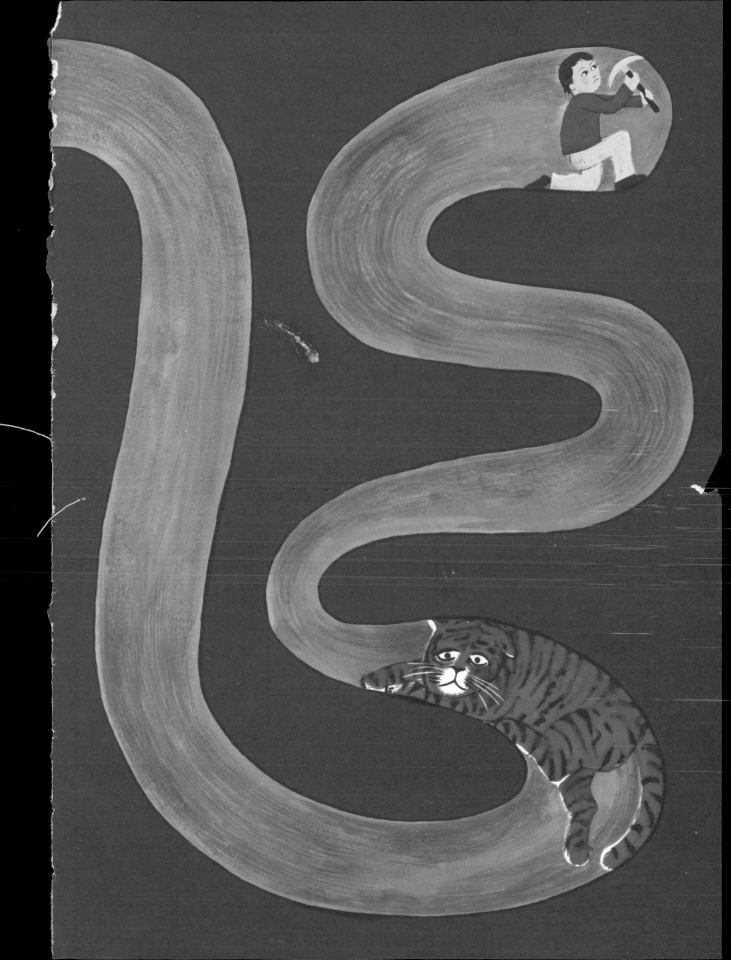

**Unfortunately
he dug himself into a fancy ballroom.**

**Fortunately
there was a surprise party going on.
And fortunately
the party was for him,
because fortunately
it was his birthday!**